The Naughty Sheep

Heather Amery

Illustrated by Stephen Cartwright

Language consultant: Betty Root
Series editor: Jenny Tyler

There is a little yellow duck to find on every page.

This is Apple Tree Farm.

This is Mrs. Boot, the farmer. She has two children, called Poppy and Sam, and a dog called Rusty.

On the farm there are seven sheep.

The sheep live in a big field with a fence around it.
One sheep has a black eye. She is called Woolly.

Woolly is bored.

Woolly stops eating and looks over the fence.
"Grass," she says, "nothing but grass. Boring."

Woolly runs out of the gate.

She runs out of the field into the farmyard. Then she runs through another gate into a garden.

Woolly sees lots to eat in the garden.

She tastes some of the flowers. "Very good,"
she says, "and much prettier than grass."

Can you see where Woolly walked?

She walks around the garden, eating lots of the flowers. "I like flowers," she says.

Mrs. Boot sees Woolly in the garden.

"What are you doing in my garden?" she shouts.
"You've eaten my flowers, you naughty sheep."

Mrs. Boot is very cross.

"It's the Show today," she says. "I was going to pick my best flowers for it. Just look at them."

It is time for the Show.

"Come on," says Poppy. "We must go now. The Show starts soon. It's only just down the road."

They all walk down the road.

Woolly watches them go. She chews her
flower and thinks, "I'd like to go to the Show."

Woolly goes to the Show.

Woolly runs down the road. Soon she comes to
a big field with lots of people in it.

Woolly goes into the ring.

She pushes past the people and into the field.
She stops by a man in a white coat.

Mrs. Boot finds her.

"What are you doing here, Woolly?" says Mrs. Boot.
"She has just won a prize," says the man.

Woolly is the winner.

"This cup is for the best sheep," says the man.
"Oh, that's lovely. Thank you," says Mrs. Boot.

It is time to go home.

"Come on, Woolly," says Mrs. Boot. "We'll take you back to your field, you naughty, clever sheep."

Cover design by Hannah Ahmed   Digital manipulation by Sarah Cronin

This edition first published in 2004 by Usborne Publishing Ltd, 83-85 Saffron Hill, London EC1N 8RT, England. www.usborne.com